Charlie's Dad

For my dad and my husband, two truly wonderful dads

© 2020 by Heather Bresett. All rights reserved.

Charlie's dad was tall with dark hair. He was known as the nicest man in town. He had nice things to say. He helped others. He was generous and liked to give away his favorite lemon drop candies that he always carried in his pocket. Everyone smiled at him and he smiled back.

Charlie wondered just what made his dad so happy.

Every Saturday morning, Charlie's dad kissed Charlie's mother goodbye and walked into town to get the groceries for the week. Sometimes he took Charlie.

One Saturday morning, when Charlie asked his mother if he could go to town with his dad, Charlie's mother said he could.

She went to a jar in the kitchen cupboard and pulled out two dollars. She handed him the money and told him to buy something special. Then she gave him a hug and a kiss.

Charlie's dad was smiling. He loved it when Charlie went to the store with him.
They left their little home by the railroad tracks.

They walked down the driveway, past the maple trees. They walked along the stone wall where the mice lived. When they reached the road, they walked on the gravel beside it.

The first person they saw was their neighbor, Harriet, sitting on her front porch. She lived two houses down.

Every Saturday, Charlie's dad would get Harriet's morning newspaper and take it to her along with a lemon drop candy.

"Dad, why do you take her the newspaper?" Charlie asked when they had left her house that morning.

"Doing nice things for the neighbors makes God happy," said Charlie's dad and he smiled.

A few blocks later, they saw something fall from the pocket of a man walking in front of them. It was a ten-dollar bill. The man's name was Mr. John. He was the school's bus driver.

"Mr. John!" Charlie's dad called out as he ran up to the man, "Mr. John, you dropped this."

The man took his money, smiled, and thanked Charlie's dad.
They kept walking and Charlie asked his dad why he gave the money to the man.

"The money is his and it would not be right to keep it. God wants us to be honest," said Charlie's dad and he smiled.

They were almost at the store when Charlie's dad burst into song. His deep voice rolled into the countryside, "Praise be to God who loves us!…"

When the song ended, Charlie asked his dad why he sang to God.

"I sing to God because he wants us to praise Him and thank Him," said Charlie's dad with a smile.

They reached the grocery store and went inside. Charlie stood on the front of the cart, his usual spot.

They bought groceries for the week. They bought milk. They bought apples. They bought eggs. Charlie's dad let Charlie pick out the ice cream. He chose vanilla, Aunt Annie's favorite. They would stop at her house on the way home. They would eat warm brownies and vanilla ice cream with Aunt Annie and Uncle Frank.

Then Charlie remembered something and he had an idea. He asked his dad to wait for him.

He went back into the store and when he walked out a few minutes later, he was smiling.

They started to walk home. The sun was shining. The birds were singing. Charlie's dad ate a lemon drop candy and he gave one to Charlie.

Little Mateo was out on his bicycle and he stopped to say hello.

Charlie's dad pulled a quarter from behind Mateo's ear and put it in his hand. "Make good use of that quarter, son," he said.

Charlie's dad stopped to talk with Farmer Bob who was brushing his horse.

He took an apple from the grocery bag. He gave it to Charlie to feed to the horse.

They reached Aunt Annie and Uncle Frank's house. They knocked but there was no answer. They heard loud voices coming from within. Charlie looked up at his dad's face. His dad looked worried.

Charlie's dad opened the door and went in. Charlie followed him.

Inside Uncle Frank was jumping around holding his burned hand. Aunt Annie was trying to calm him down.

Charlie's dad knew just what to do. He opened the bag of groceries and removed the carton of vanilla ice cream. He took Uncle Frank's hand and held the cold carton to Uncle Frank's burn. His hand began to feel better right away.

They did not have brownies that day. Instead they had the last four lemon drop candies in Charlie's dad's pocket.

Charlie's dad said a prayer for Uncle Frank to feel better soon.
Charlie asked his dad why he prayed to God.
"God wants us to trust that he will take care of us," said Charlie's dad and he smiled.

When they got home, Charlie's mother hugged and kissed Charlie. Charlie took a chocolate rose out of his pocket for his mother. He had purchased it with the money she had given him.

For his dad, he took out a new bag of lemon drop candies.

Charlie's dad asked what the chocolate flower and the candies were for.

"God wants us to be good to our parents and to love them," Charlie said and he smiled.

Charlie's dad smiled and gave Charlie a warm and tight hug and said, "And this is for you because I love you too."

And then Charlie understood why his dad smiled so much. Charlie's dad loved God and those around him and it made him happy to make God happy.

Biblical References for Discussion

"If you keep my commands, you will remain in my love, just as I have kept my Father's commands and remain in His love." John 15:10

Love for Neighbors

"Teacher, which is the greatest commandment in the Law?"

Jesus replied: "'Love the Lord your God with all your heart and with all your soul and with all your mind.' This is the first and greatest commandment. And the second is like it: 'Love your neighbor as yourself.'" Matthew 22:36-39

Honesty and Integrity

"Good will come to those who are generous and lend freely, who conduct their affairs with justice." Psalm 112:5

"Do to others as you would have them do to you." Luke 6:31

Worship/Praise

"Worship the Lord your God, and his blessing will be on your food and water. I will take away sickness from among you." Exodus 23:25

"Let everything that has breath praise the Lord. Praise the Lord." Psalm 150:6

Honor Parents

"Honor your father and your mother, as the Lord your God has commanded you, so that you may live long and that it may go well with you in the land the Lord your God is giving you." Deuteronomy 5:16

About the Author

Heather Bresett was born in Maine into a family of teachers, writers, artists, and craftsmen. She enjoys writing, painting, and dabbling in entrepreneurship.

She currently resides in Aroostook County with her husband and beautiful children who are an inspiration for children's stories and her best critics.